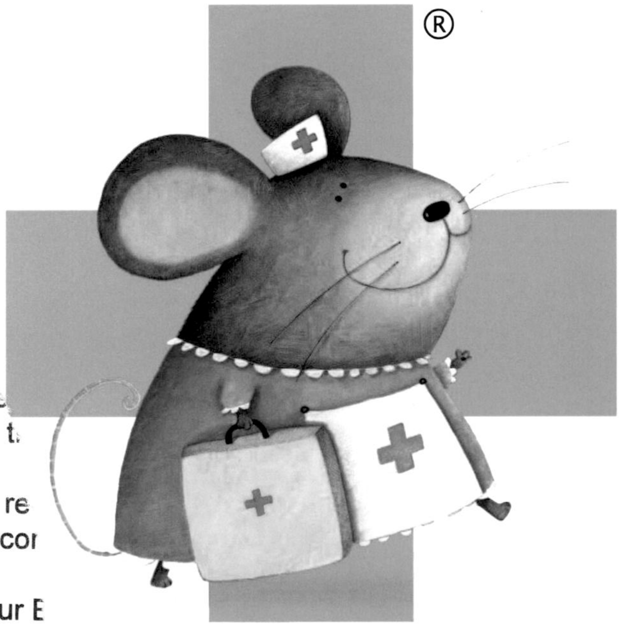

Emo the Elephant
Beyonce the Bear
Nurse Nibbles
Momo the Monkey
Pepe the Puppy
Giselle the Giraffe